T0199043

To order additional copies of this book, contact:
Xlibris
844-714-8691
www.Xlibris.com
Orders@Xlibris.com

ISBN: 978-1-6641-4592-4 (sc)
ISBN: 978-1-6641-4591-7 (e)

Print information available on the last page

Rev. date: 12/03/2020

Fennie the friendly fish and the five little frogs

A Story by Lilian Malaeb-Ajeeb, PhD

Once upon a time, there was a little fish
That lived in a big lake and had a small wish
To be in peace wherever she goes
And be good friends with those she knows

The fish's name was Fennie
She worked hard to make some money
Selling cake that she would bake
To other fish living in the lake

All day she cooks to fill her baskets
With delicious cakes, rusks and biscuits
All night shipping them east and west
Before going home to get some rest

One morning, as she took her nap
Five noisy frogs appeared in a snap
Splashing water everywhere
Shouting here and jumping there

Fennie wanted to talk to them
But did not want to cause a problem
Fennie was so tired, so she fell back asleep
As the frogs continued to yell and leap

They came back everyday
They were there just to play
Fennie decided to ask them to stop
The frogs near her were about to hop

So, she quickly went ahead
'Excuse me', to them she said
'I'm trying to get some sleep here
So, kindly quite down my dear

The lake is very deep and wide
You can go play on the other side'
But two frogs said: 'No!
Why would you sleep now?

Look at this beautiful sunlight
Enjoy it now and sleep at night
We're not going anywhere
You can go sleep over there

This gorgeous lake is all ours
And we'll play for few more hours'
Fennie slowly went back
And sadly began to pack

She took her stuff and left her home
Crying as she swam through the foam
Leaving to the other side of the water
Meanwhile, two other frogs told their mother

Learning what happened, mother frog was upset
She said, 'these two frogs have lots to learn yet
I wish I know where this fish is to apologize'
And she called the frogs: 'come here guys

We're moving to the other side of the lake
You should be ashamed of the noise you make'
All the frogs packed quickly and jumped away
Not knowing that Fennie also went that way

They started to shout and play around
Near the new house that Fennie has found
Fennie was again mad and sad
And left her new house feeling bad

'Why did they follow her?
Couldn't they just stay there?'
She asked herself and was getting angry
Feeling also tired and hungry

She soon saw a hanging piece of food
And went to grab it as fast as she could
Suddenly she was strongly pulled ahead
Something forced her to go up instead

And there was no meal anymore!
She then saw the frogs she met before
Fennie angrily shouted: 'It's you again!'
'Sorry', the frogs said but let us explain

'Explain what?' Fennie cried out
'All you do is push and shout
All this happened because of you
What other mischief do you plan to do

You caused me to leave my place
And now I'm stuck here in the face'
'No', one of the frogs replied
'We came to this other side

Because you asked us to
We didn't know you moved here too
Watch out for the hidden hooks in the bay
Please calm down and slip away'

Fennie understood! she was saved by the frogs
She started crying and gave them big warm hugs

The mother frog smiled and slowly turned
'These little ones' lesson has been learned
Dear fish, please excuse us
For all the mess we caused and fuss

And for all the harm we caused you honey'
'No, you have just saved me!' said Fennie
'I would like to be friends ever after
And share with you lots of laughter'

And so they became friends together
Caring and helping one another
The lake became a better place for everyone
To work and play and have much fun!

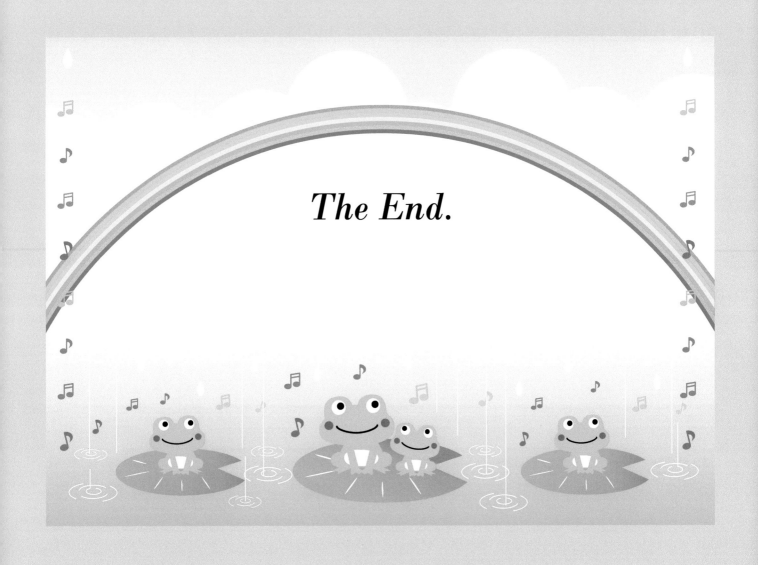

The End.

Printed in the United States
By Bookmasters